For Shale and Ever. Always remember,
a single idea can change everything.

~Dad

With thanks to my friends, who
always support me and my work.

~Mae Besom

WHAT DO YOU DO WITH AN IDEA?

Written by Kobi Yamada 🖋 Illustrated by Mae Besom

One day, I had an idea.

"Where did it come from? Why is it here?"
I wondered, "What do you do with an idea?"

At first, I didn't think much of it. It seemed kind of strange and fragile. I didn't know what to do with it. So I just walked away from it.

I acted like it didn't belong to me.

But it followed me.

I worried what others would think.
What would people say about my idea?

I kept it to myself. I hid it away and didn't talk about it.
I tried to act like everything was the same as it was
before my idea showed up.

But there was something magical about my idea. I had
to admit, I felt better and happier when it was around.

It wanted food. It wanted to play.
Actually, it wanted a lot of attention.

It grew bigger. And we became friends.

I showed it to other people even though I was afraid of
what they would say. I was afraid that if people saw it, they
would laugh at it. I was afraid they would think it was silly.

And many of them did. They said it was no good. They said it was too weird. They said it was a waste of time and that it would never become anything.

And, at first, I believed them. I actually thought about giving up on my idea. I almost listened to them.

But then I realized, what do they really know? This is MY idea, I thought. No one knows it like I do. And it's okay if it's different, and weird, and maybe a little crazy.

I decided to protect it, to care for it. I fed it good food. I worked with it, I played with it. But most of all, I gave it my attention.

My idea grew and grew.
And so did my love for it.

I built it a new house, one with an open roof where it could look up at the stars—a place where it could be safe to dream.

I liked being with my idea. It made me feel more alive,
like I could do anything. It encouraged me to think big...
and then, to think bigger.

It shared its secrets with me. It showed me how to walk on my hands. "Because," it said, "it is good to have the ability to see things differently."

I couldn't imagine my life without it.

Then, one day, something amazing happened. My idea changed right before my very eyes. It spread its wings, took flight, and burst into the sky.

I don't know how to describe it, but it went from being here to being everywhere. It wasn't just a part of me anymore… it was now a part of everything.

And then, I realized what you do with an idea...

You change the world.

COMPENDIUM.
live inspired

WITH SPECIAL THANKS TO THE ENTIRE COMPENDIUM FAMILY.

CREDITS:

Written by: Kobi Yamada

Illustrated by: Mae Besom

Designed by: Sarah Forster

Edited by: M.H. Clark & Amelia Riedler

Creative Direction by: Julie Flahiff

Library of Congress Control Number: 2013937567

ISBN: 978-1-938298-07-3

8th printing. Printed in China with soy inks. A011604008